The Emperor of Absurdia

For Jack

First published 2006 by Macmillan Children's Books
This edition published 2018 by Macmillan Children's Books
an imprint of Pan Macmillan
20 New Wharf Road, London N1 9RR
Associated companies throughout the world
www.panmacmillan.com

ISBN: 978-1-5290-0584-4

Text and illustrations copyright © Chris Riddell 2006
Moral rights asserted.

1 3 5 7 9 8 6 4 2

A CIP catalogue record for this book is available from the British Library.

Printed in China

The
Emperor
of
Absurdia

Chris Riddell

MACMILLAN CHILDREN'S BOOKS

The Emperor of Absurdia was having the most extraordinary dream. All of a sudden he woke to the hoots of the sky fish nibbling the umbrella trees.

He tumbled

out of

bed . . .

7

. . . into the arms of the
Wardrobe Monster.

The Wardrobe Monster
helped the Emperor
get dressed — in a
bobbly hat, a crumply
coat, and a pair of
jingle-jangle socks.

"Have you seen my snuggly scarf anywhere?" the Emperor asked. The Wardrobe Monster shook his big hairy head. "That's funny, I had it yesterday," said the Emperor, and set off on a scarf hunt . . .

. . . which took quite some time.

"It's no good," said the Emperor, sitting under a pointy tree. "I can't find my snuggly scarf anywhere." Just then, from the top of the tree, there came a loud, pointy-sounding squawk.

The Emperor climbed the pointy tree and found a pointy nest . . . and there was his snuggly scarf.

The Emperor of Absurdia put on his scarf and went to his high chair.

Breakfast was served.

And then supper,   followed by lunch . . .

. . . which hatched . . . and flew away.

"This is exciting!" said the Emperor.

The Emperor of Absurdia called for his tricycle
chair and set off on a dragon hunt . . .

15

. . . which took quite some time. He looked in
the flower beds and up the umbrella trees.

He looked under the pillow hills and over
the bouncy mountains.

"It's no good," said the Emperor,
climbing down from his tricycle chair.
"I can't find the little dragon anywhere."

He was just about to
give up, when he noticed
the footprints.

They led into a deep,
dark cave.

The Emperor took off his bobbly hat and his
jingle-jangle socks and put them in the pocket
of his crumply coat. Then, as quietly as he could,
he tiptoed inside the cave.

And out again!

"Help!" cried the Emperor. "An emperor hunt!"

The dragon chased the Emperor across the bouncy mountains

and through the pillow hills,

under the umbrella trees and towards the flower beds.

Then, just as the dragon was about to gobble the Emperor up, there came a loud, pointy-sounding squawk and a pointy bird swooped down and caught hold of the Emperor's scarf.

As they flew over the flower beds, the Emperor let go of the scarf and tumbled down through the air . . .

into the arms of the Wardrobe Monster.

He was so pleased to see the Emperor that he gave him an extra big hug. "I'll look for my snuggly scarf tomorrow," said the Emperor, and the Wardrobe Monster nodded his big hairy head.

Then, as a big buttercup moon rose in the sky,
the Emperor of Absurdia tumbled into bed
and fell fast asleep.

And as the sky fish snored in the umbrella trees . . .

. . . he had the most extraordinary dream.